The Pet Of
Frankenstein

More Devilish Fun with C.D. Bitesky, Howie Wolfner, Elisa and Frankie Stein, and Danny Keegan
From Avon Camelot

M Is For Monster
Born To Howl
There's A Batwing In My Lunchbox

The Pet Of Frankenstein

Mel Gilden

Illustrated by John Pierard

A GLC BOOK

AN AVON CAMELOT BOOK

THE PET OF FRANKENSTEIN is an original publication of Avon Books. This work has never before appeared in book form.

AVON BOOKS
A division of
The Hearst Corporation
105 Madison Avenue
New York, New York 10016

Text and illustrations copyright © 1988 by General Licensing Company, Inc.
Published by arrangement with General Licensing Company, Inc.
Library of Congress Catalog Card Number: 87-91678
ISBN: 0-380-75185-2
RL: 5.4

Developed by Byron Preiss and Dan Weiss
Edited by Ruth Ashby
Front cover painting by Steve Fastner and John Pierard

First Avon Camelot Printing: February 1988

Printed in the U.S.A.

OPM 10 9 8 7 6 5 4 3 2 1

Chapter One

Monsterland

The full moon rose, illuminating the Mummy and the Gillman as they confronted each other in the swamp's steamy depths. The Mummy was a disgusting mass of dirty bandages who lurched along with a pronounced limp. The Gillman was a slick green creature with fins down his arms, back, and legs. The gills at his neck flapped open and shut as he labored to breathe air, which was so much thinner than water.

The two monsters met and grappled, making horrible, unearthly cries as they thrashed around, raising fetid odors from the churning water, disturbing nightmare creatures sleeping on tangled branches or in spongy bogs. At last the Gillman lifted the Mummy high in the air and flung him away. Without a struggle, the Mummy sank beneath the scummy water.

"Elisa won," Barbara Keegan cried. She had been standing silently behind her older brother, Danny, and her friend, Elisa Stein, as they manipulated the two monsters on the video screen of the lunch box-sized game. Now she jumped up and down as she clutched her Snuggly Mutt, Doc.

1

A Snuggly Mutt was a soft plush animal with a soulful, cute, ugly face and long floppy ears. The commercial on TV said that Snuggly Mutts were just right for hugging. Barbara evidently agreed.

Though she was in the fourth grade and considered herself very grown-up, Barbara had badgered her father into buying her a Snuggly Mutt. She'd had it for about a week. During that time, she had not let the thing out of her hands except to go to school—and getting her to let go for school had been a battle. Danny was not sympathetic. He thought the entire concept of plush animals was pretty disgusting.

At the moment, however, Danny had more important things on his mind than Snuggly Mutts. He was studying Monsterland, the game Frankie Stein had invented. It was lots of fun to play, but right now there seemed to be something wrong with it.

Danny frowned and shook his head. "Elisa hasn't won yet," he said. "Here he comes again." He and Elisa and Barbara leaned forward to watch the video screen as the Mummy lurched into the picture from one side. He seemed to float over the water, dragging one leg behind him.

"The Mummy can't fly," said Barbara. "That's not fair."

"I'm not doing it," Danny said placidly. It seemed to him that the Mummy's new and unexpected ability to fly could definitely be an advantage. "Do you want to stop?" he asked Elisa.

Elisa said, "Let us proceed and see what happens."

Danny nodded and cried, "Grab the Gillman."

On the screen, the Mummy reached down and grabbed the Gillman under the arms.

"Twist around," Elisa said.

On the screen, the Gillman twisted in place as if he were fighting the Mummy's grip. Suddenly the screen went blank, leaving behind a luminous spot that rapidly faded to nothing. Barbara groaned. The speaker on the side of the game said, "Fatal Error #1016-C."

"I thought something was wrong," Elisa said. "The Mummy should not have returned after being defeated."

"He shouldn't have flown either," Barbara said, playfully punching Danny in the shoulder. Danny made a grab for her Snuggly Mutt, and Barbara backed away, shrieking with laughter.

Elisa called to her brother across the Stein's Mad Room. "Frankie?"

The Mad Room was a huge place. Enough video games to outfit the average arcade stood against one wall. In another part of the room, ranks of computers and printers waited.

Frankie was off in the home entertainment corner with Howie Wolfner. Frankie was taller than most kids his age and, like his sister, had a knob protruding from either side of his neck.

Frankie and Howie were not watching the big screen TV or listening to the compact disc player. Frankie was adjusting the dials and switches of the random tone generator while Howie sat in a big overstuffed chair with his eyes closed, his massive head of hair mashed down by the earphones he was wearing. He was smiling with delight.

"What is it?" Frankie said.

"Monsterland," Elisa said. "Fatal Error #1016-C."

"Ach," said Frankie as if he'd expected to hear this. He laid the control board of the tone generator in Howie's lap. Without opening his eyes, Howie began to alter the adjustments.

Frankie joined Danny and Barbara and his sister. He picked up the game in both hands and Frankie said, "Ready input."

"Ready," Monsterland said.

Frankie shut his eyes, and sparks jumped between his fingertips and the case of the game. The static electricity made Danny's hair stand on end. Seconds later, Frankie said, "Status?"

Monsterland said, "Nominal."

Frankie handed Monsterland back to Elisa and said, "It just needed some adjustment." He stroked Barbara's Snuggly Mutt and said, "Are you sure you will not allow me to study Doc?"

Barbara pulled the Snuggly Mutt out of Frankie's reach and said, "I know what you mean when you say 'study.' You want to take Doc apart. But we won't let him, will we, Doc?"

The Snuggly Mutt barked.

Frankie shook his head in wonder. "It is able to recognize your voice and to bark. I am just curious to compare the brain chip of your toy with the central processing unit of my Monsterland."

"No," Barbara said emphatically.

"It would not hurt," said Frankie.

"Hah!" Barbara said. "Let's see if removing *your* brain chip hurts."

"Would you care to play a round?" Elisa said to

Barbara. She pointed to the swamp on the Monsterland screen. Barbara clutched her Snuggly Mutt to her chest and sat down in the chair Danny had just vacated. Pointedly ignoring Frankie, she said, "Mrs. Bumpo really ought to give us a Girls' Pathfinders merit badge for playing this."

"I believe," Elisa said, "that at the moment Mrs. Bumpo is more interested in our getting a Public Service merit badge than one for playing video games."

"Playing a video game takes just as much skill as helping old people cross the street. We ought to be able to get a merit badge for it."

Elisa and Barbara seemed to have forgotten the game. They ignored the screen while they sat discussing what Mrs. Bumpo could possibly have in mind for them to do to earn their Public Service merit badges.

Meanwhile Danny accompanied Frankie back to the home entertainment corner. As they stood watching Howie manipulate the controls of the tone generator, Danny said, "Where's C.D.?"

Frankie said, "He is working for his uncle this afternoon."

"Too bad. He's missing Monsterland."

Frankie said, "Each of us plays his own version of Monsterland all the time."

Danny supposed that this was true. It was odd, but lately his best friends in the world were monsters. Frankie and Elisa seemed to have some of the same characteristics as the original Frankenstein's monster. Howie turned into a werewolf at will, which wasn't so bad, but also during thunderstorms, which could be very inconvenient. C.D. Bitesky seemed to be some kind of vampire.

He never ate food, just sipped on his red Fluid of Life. He even had permission to drink it during Ms. Cosgrove's fifth grade class. But they were all nice kids, nicer than some of the kids who were supposedly "normal."

Danny pulled an earphone away from one of Howie's slightly pointed, slightly hairy ears and said, "How you doing?"

Howie looked up at him with surprise, beamed, and said, "Capital, actually. Want to try it?"

"Sure." Danny took the earphones from Howie and listened. The box was indeed generating tones—the sort of noise an electronic bird might make if it were not feeling well. "Just sounds like noise to me," Danny said as he hastily took the earphones off. Howie put them on again immediately.

Elisa and Barbara strolled over. Elisa said, "I am hungry. Is anyone else?"

Danny raised his hand as if he were in school, and shook it in Elisa's face. "Me! Me!" he said.

"I will find out what we have," Frankie said, and walked to the built-in intercom. He pushed a button next to the grill and was about to speak when he stopped and listened. Danny heard Dr. and Mrs. Stein having a conversation.

"Crossed wires," Frankie said. He was about to push the button again, when something his father said caught his attention. It was hard to tell with the easygoing Frankie, but he seemed to get more upset the longer he listened.

"You think they will have to go, then?" Mrs. Stein said.

7

"Well, you must admit that the present generation does not seem quite so bright as earlier ones."

"True. And certainly size is no indication of quality. That one in particular seems rather pale in comparison. Still, it is a pity. One gets so used to having them around. Is there anything we can do?" Mrs. Stein sounded genuinely concerned.

"Oh," said Dr. Stein offhandedly, "I could always do a little engineering."

Frankie pushed the button and backed away from the intercom. He dropped into a chair in front of a computer terminal and gazed ahead, not seeing anything. "Frankie," Elisa cried. "What is wrong?"

There was a long silence during which Frankie did not move. Howie noticed that something was up. He took off his earphones and joined the group around Frankie. Like the others, he waited, unnaturally quiet. Danny knew that big stuff was going on here, and he suspected the others knew it, too.

"You heard. What are your conclusions?" Frankie spoke in a flat voice.

"My conclusions?" Elisa said with surprise. "Mama and Papa are unhappy with something." She brightened suddenly and said, "Do you think we can help?"

"You do not understand. What they are not happy with is us. With me in particular."

Elisa seemed stunned.

"This is preposterous," Howie said.

"Sure it is," Danny said. "What Howie said. You're a great guy, Frankie." Barbara nodded. She made her Snuggly Mutt nod, too.

Frankie shook his head. "You do not have all the

data. Yesterday Papa spoke to me about my low grades in school. I explained that I have not been studying so much because I have been building Monsterland, but he did not consider this a good excuse. Now I know he thinks I am not so bright as earlier generations."

"He still could have been talking about anything," Elisa said.

"Yes?" Frankie said and looked at Elisa, eyebrows raised in question.

"Certainly." Elisa thought for a moment. "Perhaps something at his work."

"No," said Frankie. "He was talking about me. He is disappointed in me. And now he is thinking of redesigning my body and reprogramming my brain."

"He said no such thing," Elisa cried.

"Of course not," Danny said. "Parents don't just go around taking their kids apart."

"For one thing," Howie said, "there are laws."

"Perhaps," Frankie said, but he didn't seem convinced. "What do *you* think he meant by 'a little engineering'?"

Even Elisa had no answer for that. But she did, however, have a very practical suggestion. She said, "Why don't we just ask them?"

"What? Mama and Papa?"

"Certainly. They can clear this whole thing up instantly."

It sounded like a good idea to Danny.

Frankie said, "I do not wish to find out for certain if I am right or wrong. For one, the fact that I may be wrong gives me some comfort. For two, if I am right, then I do not wish to remind them of this subject. They may decide to make modifications now." Frankie stood up. "No, I must prove to them that I am as good a scientist as Papa, as good even as my great-granduncle once removed, the Baron Frankenstein himself!"

"Is this a good idea?" Danny said.

Howie said, "I wasn't aware there even *was* a real Baron Frankenstein."

"It is," Frankie said, "and there was."

Elisa looked at him worriedly. She said, "You must do this?"

Frankie nodded.

"Well then," said Howie, "we're all with you."

Everyone agreed, and Frankie solemnly shook hands all around. At Barbara's insistence, he even shook Doc's paw.

Chapter Two

Invitation to the Weird

In school the next day, Frankie looked more worried than usual. Once Elisa tried to pat his hand comfortingly, but Frankie pulled away. When Ms. Cosgrove asked him to tell her the circumference of the earth, he told her the radius instead. If any other student had made this mistake, it would have meant nothing. But a mistake like that from Frankie meant that his mind was definitely somewhere else.

Later, while the class was answering the questions in the back of the Earth Science chapter of their science book, Ms. Cosgrove called Frankie up to her desk.

All the kids liked Ms. Cosgrove. It was true, she was very pretty. But more importantly, she was very nice. This did not mean she was easy. Almost everybody worked harder for her and learned more from her than they did with any other teacher, mainly because she was so enthusiastic about everything. The enthusiasm was infectious. Some of the boys even went all mushy when they talked about her outside of school.

Still, being called on for a private conference with

any teacher was upsetting. As he lumbered across the room, Frankie accidentally knocked into Marla Willaby's desk. Marla fluttered her eyelashes at him. Frankie mumbled, "Excuse me," but paid no attention to the eyelashes. Marla did stuff like that all the time. She changed boyfriends more often than some guys changed their socks.

Danny tried to do his Earth Science questions and at the same time figure out what Ms. Cosgrove was saying to Frankie. He had more luck with the questions than with the spy work.

At first recess, Frankie refused to get involved in any of the games. "No great loss," said Stevie Brickwald in a nasty tone of voice. This was not unusual. He usually spoke in a nasty tone of voice.

Danny agreed that Frankie was not much of an athlete, but he tried hard and did his best, and there were many kids who'd rather have Frankie Stein on their team than Stevie Brickwald.

Frankie and Elisa stood under a tree in the far corner of the school yard. They both looked worried now. Elisa appeared to be doing all the talking. Whether Frankie was listening or not, Danny could not say.

C.D. often spent recess and lunchtime in the tree under which Frankie and Elisa were standing. Actually, if a person who had very good eyes looked in just the right place up in that tree, he or she might see a bat hanging upside down from one of the stouter branches.

Danny knew that bat was C.D. He'd seen C.D. change form lots of times. He'd not yet gotten used to it, but there was no question that it happened.

Even as Danny and Howie approached, the bat in the

tree dropped, and like a big black umbrella opening, turned into C.D. just before it hit the ground. As usual, C.D. was wearing his tuxedo. He adjusted his bow tie and took a thermos from a pocket inside his cape. He pulled a straw from the thermos and took a long draw on the Fluid of Life.

When he released the straw from his mouth, C.D. said to Frankie, "You do not look well, my friend." C.D. spoke in a rolling Transylvanian accent.

Elisa said, "Has not anyone told you what happened over the weekend?"

"Not anyone."

Before Elisa could explain Frankie's problem, Danny and Howie walked up. Danny said, "So, what did Ms. Cosgrove have to say?"

"Not very much," Frankie said.

Elisa said, "Perhaps I can tell them?"

Frankie gave a small nod.

"Actually, she said exactly what you would expect. She is concerned for Frankie's welfare."

"I can't blame her," Howie said. He reached up and laid a hand on Frankie's shoulder. "We all are."

"Perhaps I might be of assistance if I knew the nature of the problem," C.D. said.

Elisa told C.D. what they had overheard on the intercom in the Mad Room of the Stein mansion, and what Frankie and Dr. Stein had discussed the day before. C.D. nodded. Then Elisa told him what Frankie had concluded from all this. Frankie sighed. C.D. nodded again and said, "Ah," as if he understood perfectly what Elisa was talking about.

"Have you spoken with your parents?" C.D. said.

Frankie explained again why this was not possible. If he didn't know the truth, he still had some hope. And if he was right about his parents' intentions, he did not want to remind them of what they had decided. Besides, he would rather disprove their opinion of him than ask for their charity. C.D. said, "Ah so," as if he no longer understood but didn't want to ask more questions.

Howie said, "Then you have not given up your attempt to prove your superiority over the Baron Frankenstein?"

Frankie shook his head. He said, "Show-and-Tell will be my first step."

"What does that mean?" Danny said.

"You will see."

"You haven't rewired the school or something, have you?" Howie said.

Frankie looked at Howie with sudden interest, as if this thought had not occurred to him, but now that it had, it was a definite possibility.

"You have not done this, I trust," C.D. said.

Frankie shook his head again.

The bell rang, ending recess. As they walked back to class Danny said to Frankie, "You don't want anybody to get hurt."

"No," Frankie said, and refused to say any more.

At last Show-and-Tell time arrived. Ms. Cosgrove seemed unaware that this particular Show-and-Tell would be any different from others she had presided over.

But Danny and the monster kids fidgeted as Arthur Finster did a magic trick involving a rubber band pulled tight across his fist. When he opened his hand, the rubber band seemed to jump from one finger to another. His father had shown the trick to him. It was a good trick, but Danny knew how to do it himself, so it lost some of its mystery.

Next, Jason Nickles tried to get somebody to look through his new telescope. "Is that a practical joke?" Ms. Cosgrove asked sternly. She had dealt with Jason before.

Jason admitted that it was and was reduced to demonstrating by looking through the telescope himself. When he took it down, it left an inky black circle around his eye. He bowed as if he'd just performed some incredible feat. The kids laughed and even Ms. Cosgrove smiled.

"Thank you, Jason," Ms. Cosgrove said. "I don't want to see that in school again. Anybody else have something to share?"

A moment went by, and Danny thought that maybe Frankie had changed his mind. Then Frankie raised his hand. Ms. Cosgrove called on him, and Frankie walked to the front of the room.

Danny kept his eye on the sink where they rinsed out their paintbrushes. He expected it to start shooting sparks at any moment.

Then Danny saw that Frankie was carrying something the size and shape of a lunch box. It was Monsterland. Danny sighed with relief. He knew what Frankie had in mind, and it was OK. C.D. still looked worried, because he had never before seen Monsterland. Danny tried to gesture to him that everything was OK.

"Do you need to use the rest room, Danny?" Ms. Cosgrove said.

The class laughed.

"No, Ms. Cosgrove." Danny slumped in his chair and waited for Frankie to make his presentation.

"This is Monsterland," Frankie said. "It is a game that I have invented myself." The students' interest quickly faded as Frankie gave them a technical explanation of how he had designed it, what sort of chips it used, and the extent of both its read-only and its random-access memories. Danny doubted if even Ms. Cosgrove understood most of it.

But Frankie grabbed his audience right back when he began to demonstrate how the game worked. He called out commands, making the Gillman, the Mummy, and a living heap of garbage called the Dump battle one another across the swamp.

"Wow!"

"Neato!"

"Radical!"

"Tubular!"

With Ms. Cosgrove's permission, Frankie asked for volunteers to play the game. Everybody in the room raised a hand. Frankie smiled.

Show-and-Tell took a little longer than usual because Ms. Cosgrove did not want to deny Monsterland to anybody. Frankie helped each kid play a couple of turns. Through it all, Frankie smiled, delighted for once to be the center of attention.

Even Stevie Brickwald took his turn and could think of nothing nasty to say. He just shrugged and said, "It's OK, I guess," and went to sit down. As far as Danny was concerned, coming from a guy like Stevie, this was a major compliment.

As usual, when school was over, Danny and the

monster kids met to talk for a few minutes before starting home. C.D. bowed in Frankie's direction and said, "I salute you and your game. You are a great scientist."

"Thank you," Frankie said. "I wish that my father would feel this way."

"Come on, Frankie," Danny said. "You think Baron Frankenstein could build a game like that? He probably didn't even know what a transistor was."

"That is hardly fair to the Baron. He lived in the nineteenth century."

There didn't seem to be any answer to that. Shortly, C.D. said, "In any case, I would delight in inviting you, Frankie, and the rest of you, too, to my home this coming Friday evening. It will be a family party."

"Capital," Howie cried. "Very kind, I'm sure."

"My Uncle Emeric will be there," C.D. went on. "He is the owner of Chiroptera Electronics, where I have been working weekends these past few weeks. I would like very much for him and Frankie to meet. And please to bring Monsterland. After seeing it, perhaps my uncle would care to hire you for something."

"To sweep floors," Frankie said morosely.

"Now now," Elisa said. "We would be delighted to attend, if you are certain we would not be intruding."

"I can assure you, all of you will be most welcome."

C.D. extended his invitation on Monday. Danny spent a lot of that long week alternately wondering what a party of C.D.'s vampire relatives would be like and watching helplessly as Frankie became more and more despondent.

Danny cornered Frankie in the bathroom and asked him if things had improved.

"There are many problems," Frankie said. As he spoke, he casually played with a drip from a water faucet.

"I'll bet C.D.'s Uncle Emeric will be able to help you."

"Maybe. Maybe I will say or do the wrong thing. Maybe he will not like Monsterland."

"You worry too much."

"I may already be spare parts by Friday. It is impossible to worry too much. But thank you for your concern." Frankie gave the drip a tiny zap with one finger, and it hissed as it vaporized. The steam was still rising as he walked away.

Danny was frustrated because he wanted to help Frankie but had no idea where to start. When he had a chance, he spoke to Elisa. They were standing at easels, each attempting to paint a picture of pioneers crossing the Great Plains.

Elisa said, "Frankie cannot decide on a project. He begins to do one thing, thinks better of it, and flings it angrily aside, only to start on something else. I believe he was working on superconductivity yesterday afternoon, but his progress did not satisfy him. In his view, nothing is grand enough to save him." Elisa glared at her painting as if it had offended her. "I am sure that the back knee of that horse is incorrect."

Danny glanced at it and said, "I think it's supposed to bend the other way. Can't you talk to your mom and dad?"

Elisa sighed. "I would like to. I have started more

than once. But the promise I gave to Frankie prevents me. Perhaps he is right about what they have in mind. I do not want to ruin his chances. Or mine either. It is true they have begun to look at Frankie strangely."

"I'm not surprised. He's not exactly the Frankie we're used to."

Danny and Elisa each painted for a while. Danny tried to fix the buffalo he was working on. At the moment, it looked like a dog. He said, "Your parents would really take Frankie apart?"

Elisa shrugged. "They put both him and me together," she said.

Danny couldn't argue with that.

It was a long time till Friday, but when it came at last, both Frankie and Elisa were still in one piece.

Chapter Three

Fangs a Lot, Uncle Emeric

Friday night was cold and crisp. The stars looked like the points of needles, the sliver of moon like a fingernail clipping caught in the empty branches of a tree in the Keegan front yard.

Danny had to wait out front of his house for only a moment before Mrs. Wolfner and Howie came by in the Wolfners' classic old station wagon with genuine wood paneling on the sides. Danny playfully punched Howie in the shoulder as he slid in next to the window. The two boys and Howie's mom all seemed like monsters, breathing smoke into the cold air.

Danny had Frankie on his mind, and from the thoughtful expression Howie had on his face, Danny figured that Howie was thinking about him, too.

But Mrs. Wolfner was an adult. Danny didn't feel right about discussing Frankie's problem in front of her. You never knew what parents might tell each other. And in the unlikely event that Frankie was right about his parents' intentions, Danny didn't want to be the one responsible for Frankie and Elisa being broken down into spare parts.

Danny and Howie talked about their paintings of pioneers. Howie said that given a choice, he, at any rate, would have preferred to skateboard from St. Louis to California rather than walk or ride in a wagon.

Danny laughed and suggested that a jumbo jet might have been more comfortable. That started a competition in which Howie and Danny each tried to be sillier than the other. Mrs. Wolfner won the competition when she suggested that the *Starship Enterprise* could have probably made the trip across country in a few seconds.

"Yeah, warp drive," Danny said.

"Which driver is warped?" said Mrs. Wolfner, and all three of them laughed.

Mrs. Wolfner drove quickly past the small dark shops in C.D.'s neighborhood. Now, at night, they looked even emptier and more forlorn than they did during the day when they were open for business. A lot of people in long dark overcoats and big hats were out walking, but there wasn't much car traffic.

The station wagon pulled up before a big old brick building, the Fisherman Arms. Danny and Howie piled out of the car, but Howie leaned back in and told his mother that he wouldn't be late.

"No matter, dear," Mrs. Wolfner said. "Your father and I will be up studying the moon this evening. Just call when you're ready to come home."

Howie nodded and Danny looked up and saw that the moon was caught in a different tree now. Good thing the moon wasn't full or Howie might be out howling and sniffing around garbage cans with his family, and he would miss the party.

Danny and Howie walked one flight down to the

22

Stitch in Time Tailoring Service. Danny shaded his eyes with one hand and looked between the wrought-iron bars through the glass pane in the door. It was so dark inside that the clothes he saw hanging from racks looked like rank on rank of monsters. "Pretty quiet for a party," Danny said. "I don't hear anything."

"Bats don't make much noise when they're just hanging around," Howie said and pushed a button next to the door. Far away, in the depths of the house—in the catacombs?—Danny heard a buzzer sound.

While they were waiting for somebody to answer the door, Danny said, "I wish you wouldn't say stuff like that." Howie just chuckled evilly and rubbed his hands together.

Seconds later, a very tall man wearing a tuxedo came to the door. Golden half-glasses were perched on the tip of his nose. Danny recognized him right away. This was Mr. Bitesky, C.D.'s father.

Mr. Bitesky licked his lips, which seemed to be redder and fuller than Danny recalled, and said, "Yes, boys? If you have come to pick up mending, I am sorry. The shop is closed."

"Uh, no, Mr. Bitesky. I'm Danny Keegan, and this is Howie Wolfner. C.D. invited us to the party. I hope that's OK."

"Of course. I remember now. Delighted," said Mr. Bitesky as he opened the door wide.

Mr. Bitesky led Danny and Howie through the dark tailor shop and along the hall hung with paintings of C.D.'s ancestors. According to C.D., most of them were still alive. Maybe they would be at the party. Danny trusted C.D. not to suck his blood, and to a lesser extent, he trusted C.D.'s parents. But could he trust ancestors who had been vampires for centuries and were used to it? The phrase *necking party* took on a whole new meaning.

As they walked, the babble of voices grew louder. Sounds just like a regular party, Danny thought, trying to give himself confidence.

They passed the painting of Castle Bitesky, and Mr. Bitesky showed the two boys into a large room lit entirely by candles. The golden candlelight made everything in the room seem to glow from within.

People stood around in groups talking. They could have been friends of Danny's parents, except all the men were wearing tuxedos and long capes and all the women wore long filmy white gowns. Each man had a thick, red satin sash covered with medals hanging diagonally across his chest.

Each of the party guests held a Styrofoam cup in one hand. Danny assumed that the cups were full of the red stuff that filled a punch bowl on the large heavy table in the center of the room. The chances were good that the red stuff was Fluid of Life, or a party version that was very much like it. Danny decided he wasn't thirsty.

Suddenly strange violin music began to throb from speakers in the corners. It made Danny think of wildly leaping men wearing kerchiefs wrapped around their heads and big gold earrings.

C.D. ran over to Danny and Howie, followed by his mother. Like the other women, she looked ghostly, not quite real, in her flowing white gown. "There you are," C.D. said joyfully.

"C.D.," Mrs. Bitesky said warningly.

C.D. glanced at his mother, then turned back to Howie and Danny. C.D. bowed and clicked his heels together and said, "I am delighted that you could come." He grabbed each of their right hands in turn and jerked it once.

"Very good," said Mrs. Bitesky. "Good evening, boys. Would you like some punch?"

Howie said, "None for me, thanks."

"Me neither," said Danny. "I'm on kind of a diet."

"Very well," said Mrs. Bitesky jovially. "Be comfortable." She wandered away to mix with her other guests.

Danny looked around the room. "I don't see Frankie or Elisa."

"They have not yet arrived. However—"

Howie interrupted. "Who is *that?*"

Danny looked into the corner across the room where Howie was pointing. Standing there, half in shadow, was a tall, grim figure. He bore the same resemblance to Mr. Bitesky as a hawk does to a sparrow. He had his cape wrapped tightly around his body, and he was glaring over the top of it with dark, piercing eyes.

"That," said C.D., "is The Count, a very old and venerable ancestor. I am named after him."

Danny thought that over for a moment. "The Count. *The* Count?" he said. "As in Drac—"

"He is The Count," C.D. said with great finality.

Danny and Howie nodded and tried not to stare.

"Come," said C.D. "I will introduce you to Uncle Emeric." As they followed C.D. across the room, Danny noticed copies of *Hemoglobin Magazine* fanned on the coffee table and shuddered. He wondered if he would ever get used to having a vampire for a friend. At the moment, Howie seemed just about normal.

Mr. Bitesky was talking to a thick round dowel of a man. He was shorter than Mr. Bitesky, but then, just about everybody was. The medals on the short man's sash looked like transistors and other electronic stuff. As they approached, Mr. Bitesky laughed at something the man said.

"Excuse me, Father," C.D. said. "Uncle Emeric, these are my friends, Danny and Howie."

"How are you?" Uncle Emeric said. He spoke sarcastically, and from the corner of his mouth, as if he were telling a private joke that he alone understood. It made Danny feel uncomfortable, as if he should have known the joke. "I hope," Uncle Emeric went on, "that you are not believing too much of what C.D. tells you about me."

"Actually," said Howie, "C.D. hasn't told us much except that you are the owner of Chiroptera Electronics."

"He is entirely correct. Which of you is the electronics genius?"

"Neither of them," C.D. said. "Frankie Stein has not yet arrived." At that moment, the buzzer rang. The sound seemed to come from someplace beneath Danny's feet. "Perhaps that is him even now." C.D. and his father left the room.

Danny and Howie stood with Uncle Emeric. Danny could think of nothing to say, but Howie asked him questions about the electronics business. As Howie and Uncle Emeric went on, Danny decided that Uncle Emeric was probably an OK guy, and that he couldn't help the strange sideways way he talked. He only hoped that Frankie would not be flustered by it.

Uncle Emeric said, "I am recently importing a new line of products from Transylvania. It will include such things as wing polish, nonlethal sunlamps, moonlamps, special high-pitched navigation beacons, electronic bat calls, and electronic programmable dowsing rods."

"Jolly good fun," Howie said. "Tell me more about the moonlamps."

Only half of Danny's attention was focused on the conversation between Howie and Uncle Emeric. The other half was on the doorway, watching to see who C.D. and Mr. Bitesky had gone to let in. Danny hoped that Frankie wasn't so worried and depressed that he'd decided not to come to the party at all. Still, it was early. Plenty of time. Everything would be OK, even if that wasn't Frankie and Elisa at the door just yet.

An age later, C.D. and Mr. Bitesky showed Frankie and Elisa Stein into the room. Danny smiled and nudged Howie and began to wave. When Howie saw Frankie and Elisa, he smiled and waved, too.

Elisa waved back. Frankie did not. He barely smiled. Evidently, the fact that he'd made it to Friday night without being disassembled had not improved his outlook on life.

Elisa had on a pretty pink dress with a black lightning bolt down one side. All that could be said for Frankie was that he was reasonably neat and clean. Colored pens lined his shirt pocket, as they usually did, and a cowlick would not stay down no matter how often he smoothed it into place with the flat of one hand. The important thing was that in his other hand, Frankie carried Monsterland.

Elisa and C.D. began to speak to him earnestly, nodding in the direction of Danny and Howie and Uncle Emeric, but Frankie kept shaking his head.

"Friends of yours?" said Uncle Emeric.

Danny said, "That's Frankie Stein, the electronics genius."

For a moment, the three of them watched Elisa and C.D. argue with Frankie. At last, Uncle Emeric said, "This is ridiculous," and strode across the room. Danny and Howie could do nothing but follow.

Uncle Emeric took Frankie's hand and shook it and introduced himself. Frankie seemed bewildered. He gaped at Uncle Emeric and at last managed to squeal, "How do you do?"

"I do fine," Uncle Emeric said. He chuckled at his little joke. "What are you carrying?"

"Uh," said Frankie, "this is Monsterland."

Elisa said, "It is a video game that my brother, Frankie, designed and built all by himself. He is a genius."

"It is true," C.D. said.

"Quite right," Howie said.

"Absolutely," Danny said.

"Many testimonials from friends mean nothing," Uncle Emeric said. "Let us see the game." He held out one hand, and Frankie gave Monsterland to him. Uncle Emeric put his other hand around Frankie's shoulder and guided him toward the couch. They sat down, and with increasing enthusiasm, Frankie explained the game to him.

Elisa, Danny, C.D., and Howie watched from across the room. Danny said, "It looks good."

"Uncle Emeric is a fine man. He will help Frankie."

C.D. said, "They will be conversing for a while. Perhaps we might amuse ourselves in my room."

"I remember your room," Danny said accusingly.

"I am sure you do," C.D. said. He led the way into the kitchen. The kids moved the kitchen table—difficult now because it carried a punch bowl full of red stuff—and opened the trapdoor. C.D. flicked a switch and light sprang up from below, illuminating a long stone staircase. He said to Danny, "We have had electric lights installed since you were last here." He began to descend.

"That's good," Danny said, but he was still not enthusiastic. He followed C.D. Howie and Elisa, more curious than frightened, came after. The footsteps of the four kids echoed.

At the bottom of the stairs was a large damp room with a ceiling supported by thick columns. The sandy floor was empty but for three widely spaced coffins.

Howie said nervously, "I don't think I like this. Not one bit."

"You'll get used to it," Danny said, "I guess."

"I think not. I like to be a little closer to nature, closer to the sky, to the moon."

"Not many people would come to Brooklyn to get closer to nature," C.D. said. "However," he said, smiling and showing his fangs, "I can certainly understand your longing for the moon."

"Indeed," Elisa said. "To each his own. Why have you brought us here, C.D.?"

The door buzzer rang, and everyone but C.D. jumped.

The loud noise seemed to fill the chamber. C.D. only nodded and said, "Another guest." He walked to one of the coffins and pulled open a drawer in its side. With his back to the others, he said, "Perhaps these would be of interest."

What would a vampire kid keep in his coffin, Danny wondered. Hypodermic needles for extracting blood? Instruments of torture? Souvenir bats? Danny stood his ground. Neither C.D. nor any of his other monster friends had ever hurt him. Danny forced himself to stop worrying.

C.D. turned around suddenly and held aloft a small cloth bag. He shook the bag and whatever was inside clinked together. Fangs waiting for the tooth fairy?

"Money?" said Howie, confused.

"Marbles," said C.D., and poured them onto the sandy floor.

C.D. drew a circle on the sandy floor, and the kids played marbles for a while. Soon, though, Elisa said, "I wonder how Frankie is."

Danny crouched down close to the floor and sighted along his shooter marble. "Uncle Emeric has probably made him a zillionaire by now." Danny flicked the shooter with his thumb and saw the marble click into three others.

They sat silently looking at the marbles for a while. It was not long before they decided to go back to the party. Danny knew that none of them was fooling anybody. They all were less interested in the party than they were in Frankie. They collected the marbles back into the bag and went upstairs.

When they arrived in the party room, Frankie was laughing. Elisa ran to the couch, and the others followed. Uncle Emeric and Frankie stood up. Frankie said, "Uncle Emeric has hired me to work on a special project for Chiroptera Electronics."

"You see?" said C.D. "I told you that Uncle Emeric would be helpful."

Elisa said, "You were correct. I am certain that Frankie will do well."

"As a matter of fact," Uncle Emeric said, "I would like to hire all of you to work on the project. All but C.D., who, of course, already works for me."

Frankie looked at Uncle Emeric, suddenly horrified. "What?"

Uncle Emeric said, "You certainly have no objections to working with your friends."

"No," said Frankie, frowning. He shook his head.

"Very well, then what do you say? I'll pay you what I'm paying C.D."

"If Frankie would rather we didn't . . ." Howie began and trailed off.

"No," Frankie said again. "It is fine. Really."

It was that "really" that convinced Danny that taking the job was not fine. Still, if Frankie wanted to pretend otherwise, he would, too. He took the job, and so did the others.

After that, neither Danny nor the other kids wanted to stay longer at the party. C.D. seemed to understand. Howie called his parents, and his mom said that she could take the Stein kids home, too.

C.D. waited with his friends for Mrs. Wolfner to arrive. They stood sheltered from the biting winter wind in the walkway beneath the street level in front of the Stitch in Time Tailoring Shop. No one talked about anything but the cold till Elisa said, "Perhaps Frankie would now like to tell us why he is suddenly so sad."

A long time seemed to pass. Smoke came from Frankie's mouth and nose in short gasps. At last he said, "I thought that C.D.'s Uncle Emeric was giving me a technical job. One I could use to prove to our parents that I am as smart as anyone in the family."

"What makes you think he is not?" C.D. said.

"You are all my friends," Frankie said, "but you will agree that you are not electronic geniuses. If Uncle Emeric is hiring all of us to do the same thing, how technical can the job be?"

"By Jove, he's right," Howie said.

"Yes," Frankie said. "Which means that I still have a problem."

Chapter Four

The Very Bats in Electronics

The next morning Danny walked down to Chiroptera Electronics. It wasn't in C.D.'s neighborhood, but in a brand-new shopping center only a few blocks from Danny's house. A sign over the front door of the store said THE VERY BATS IN ELECTRONICS.

Howie, Frankie, Elisa, and C.D. were already there, standing near the cash register. Or at least Frankie, Elisa, and C.D. were there. Howie was wandering around the store, exclaiming over the electronic gadgets.

"How are you doing, big guy?" Danny said to Frankie.

"I am still in one piece."

"Frankie and I are fine," Elisa said. "We are ready to start work."

Uncle Emeric strode from his office at the back of the store. He greeted them casually and then took them to a set of metal double doors. He said, "Through there is my storage room. In the center of the room is a large unopened crate from Transylvania. You will please to unpack it, stuff the packing material into large plastic bags you will find, and throw them into the dumpster.

You will neatly stack the new products on shelves. OK?''

"Quite," said Howie.

"This means yes?" said Uncle Emeric.

"It does," said Elisa.

"Good. If you have questions, visit me and C.D. in my office. Do not bring packing material with you." Uncle Emeric marched off with C.D.

"I wonder why he's such a bug on that packing material," Howie said as he pushed through the double doors. Danny, Elisa, and Frankie were right behind him. The storage room was filled with cardboard boxes, open crates of electronic components, and coils of wire. As promised, in the center of the room was a crate that was almost as tall as Danny. On the side were stenciled the words PRODUCT OF TRANSYLVANIA, followed by a silhouette of a bat with fangs.

"Pretty funny," Danny said.

"Pretty silly," Howie said and scratched under one arm. "Well, let's begin."

Howie grabbed a crowbar lying nearby and began to pry the top off the crate. Once he got the top up a little, the other kids helped him pull it off all the way. "Watch it," Howie said angrily. "Watch it."

Howie threw the crowbar to the floor with a clang and cried, "You stupid people keep getting in my way!" He was scratching like mad now. He pulled some packing material from the crate. His eyes went glassy as he threw it into the air.

"Uh-oh," said Danny as he jumped back.

Howie crouched down and howled so loudly the metal beams in the ceiling vibrated. Quickly his nose and ears

36

lengthened. Hair grew all over his face, arms, and hands. He galloped around, howling, knocking things over, stopping occasionally to sniff at something, then continuing on.

"What happened?" Danny cried.

As she danced out of Howie's way, Elisa said, "Must be that something in the crate turned him into a werewolf."

"The question is," said Frankie, "how do we stop him?"

"Get him out of the storage room," cried a new voice.

Elisa, Frankie, and Danny turned to see C.D. standing at the door. "Get him out of here," C.D. cried again.

But Howie was way ahead of him. Still running on all fours, he nearly knocked C.D. over as he banged through the double doors and into the store.

"Not in there," cried C.D. as he leaped after Howie.

Howie scrambled up shelves, scattering boxes of tiny electronic components all over the floor. "No, Howie!" C.D. cried. "Bad dog!"

Uncle Emeric ran out of his office and saw what was going on. He shook C.D. by the shoulders and frantically asked, "Why did you not tell me one of your friends was a werewolf?"

While C.D. looked for a good answer, Frankie began to run around the store. But instead of chasing Howie, he collected various bits of electronic equipment off the shelves, then went to a counter and quickly began to wire it all together with alligator clips.

"Anybody got a hot dog?" Danny said, remembering the calming effect they had on Howie.

"We have no need of hot dogs," Frankie said. He flicked a switch on his makeshift machine, and a wavering musical tone filled the air. Howie paid no attention.

Under Frankie's control, the tone changed and exploded into the songs of hundreds of mechanical birds. Howie sat down on a jumble of setscrews and capacitors and cocked an ear in Frankie's direction. He howled along with the birdsong, stopped momentarily to scratch behind his ear with one foot, and began again.

"That is doing it," Uncle Emeric said in wonderment.

"Of course," said Elisa. "Frankie is an electronics genius."

Uncle Emeric nodded.

As Frankie continued to play his tone generator, Howie yawned, turned around three times in place, curled up on the floor, and went to sleep. Seeing this, Frankie began to take his machine apart.

"He will be fine now," C.D. said. He looked at Danny. "What began his transformation?"

"I think," said Elisa, "that it was something in the crate we were unpacking." She and everyone else looked at Uncle Emeric.

Uncle Emeric kept an eye on Howie while he said, "The shipment comes from Transylvania. It is packed in garlic and wolfsbane to keep it safe."

"You should have told me," C.D. said.

"You should have told me your friend was a werewolf," Uncle Emeric said.

There was no denying that both of them were right. Danny thought that C.D. and Uncle Emeric were going

39

to have an argument. They glared at each other for a moment, but then, much to Danny's surprise, only bowed to each other politely. C.D. said, "I hope that this will not mean termination for Howie."

"Termination?" said Danny worriedly. When a bad guy on television talked about termination, it usually meant a swift and unpleasant end for his victim.

"Fear not," Uncle Emeric said. "Howie will work with us in the office. I trust that none of your other friends has—how shall I say it?—special needs?"

C.D. shared glances with Frankie and Elisa, obviously trying to decide if Uncle Emeric needed to know that they were monster kids, too.

Elisa said, "We are fine, thank you, Uncle Emeric."

"Of course," Uncle Emeric said, as if he did not believe a word of it. "Let us straighten the stock. I want everything as it was by the time we open in half an hour. Understand?"

"Yes, Uncle Emeric."

"How long will Howie sleep?"

"Only a few minutes," Danny said.

"Very good. It is only right that he help us."

Frankie was not very good at putting things away neatly. But he was a real whiz at knowing what things were and where they went. Uncle Emeric observed all this and smiled, but he did not comment on it.

When Howie awoke, he was embarrassed by the mess he had made, and he dug in to help with a will. Working quickly, he scooped up parts and under Frankie's direction got them back into their proper boxes. Trying to prove how sorry he was, he worked faster than any of the other kids. They finished straightening the store and even had a few minutes to spare before the doors opened.

Uncle Emeric nodded and said, "Is good! Howie, come with C.D. and me. The rest of you please to unpack the crate and be *very* careful with the packing material." He winked knowingly, turned abruptly, and walked to his office with C.D. and Howie in his wake.

Danny, Elisa, and Frankie returned to the storage room. It was a mess, too, and the three of them did their best to organize things before they went back to unpacking the crate. They were very careful with the packing material.

Inside the crate, they found many of the things Uncle Emeric had told Howie about at the party the night before. Wing polish came in flat cans like shoe polish. Electronic bat calls looked like whistles with sparkling rhinestone buttons. Programmable dowsing rods looked more like transistor radios.

"What are the dowsing rods for?" Danny said. Strangely enough, the uses of the wing polish and the bat whistles seemed obvious. He shook his head. He'd been around these monster kids too long.

Elisa read the side of the box. "It says 'Useful for finding lost objects such as a bag of native soil that may have been misplaced.' "

"Sure," said Danny. "Why not? What would a coffin be without some nice native soil?"

"C.D. and his family might say that without native soil, a coffin was just a box," Elisa said reprovingly.

"Right," Danny said. "Sorry. I'm beginning to sound like Stevie Brickwald." He clunked himself on the side of his head with the palm of one hand as if to shake his brains loose. He and Elisa laughed.

Elisa stopped laughing abruptly and looked closely at something that Frankie had just brought out of the crate. It was a cardboard tube about the size of a can of soup. "What is it?" Elisa said as she stared over her brother's shoulder.

"It says 'Enclosed is your free gift—a thank-you for purchasing $1000 worth or more of merchandise from The Transylvania Export Company. We appreciate your patronage.' " He shook the package. Something solid knocked from end to end.

"Open it," said Danny excitedly.

"Perhaps we should allow Uncle Emeric that privilege," Elisa said.

"Good idea. Let's take it to him."

Frankie nodded and lumbered out of the storeroom. Elisa and Danny followed him into Uncle Emeric's office.

The office was a small room, entirely lined with filing cabinets. Transylvanian and Rumanian travel posters had been taped to the walls. Howie and C.D. stood behind a big beaten-up desk in the center of the room sorting a huge pile of paper into smaller piles.

"Where's Uncle Emeric?" said Danny.

"Out helping a customer," C.D. said. "Is there a problem?"

Frankie showed them the thing he'd found in the crate. Burning with curiosity, C.D. took the package and carried it out onto the sales floor. Danny and the others were not far behind.

The kids waited impatiently while Uncle Emeric rang

up a sale and handed a small paper bag to a man dressed in a business suit. Uncle Emeric said, "I am certain this will solve the problem with your stereo." The man nodded, thanked him, and left.

"Well, what is it?" Uncle Emeric said.

"Frankie found this in the crate," C.D. said and handed the tube to Uncle Emeric.

"This is no big deal," Uncle Emeric said. "You may open it." He handed the tube back to C.D., who handed it to Frankie, who took it eagerly.

"Open it. Open it," Danny said.

"Are you positive there is no packing material in there?" Howie said. He was only half-kidding.

Frankie found a tab and pulled it sharply. The end of the tube tore off all at once and flew across the room. "I will get it soon," Frankie mumbled as he poured the contents of the tube into his hand.

Inside the tube was another tube. It seemed to be made of hard wax and had grooves wound tightly around it. One end had a cardboard cover that said MARY HAD A LITTLE LAMB. Below that, in larger letters, it said THOMAS EDISON. Below that, in much smaller letters, it said 1877.

"What is it?" Danny said.

"I have heard of these," said Elisa. "It is a cylinder for use with an Edison Recording Machine. This cylinder has Edison himself reading 'Mary Had a Little Lamb' recorded on it."

"Jolly good," Howie exclaimed. "Is it authentic?"

"Perhaps," said Uncle Emeric. "I believe the Transylvanian Export Company makes no claims either way."

"Very interesting," Frankie said as he inspected the cylinder. "You have more of these?"

"You are getting an idea?" Elisa said.

"Perhaps," Frankie said.

Uncle Emeric said, "I order much from the Transylvanian Export Company. They send me many gifts— things for which I have no use."

"May I see them?" Frankie said.

Uncle Emeric shrugged and took them to his office, where he pulled a big box from under his desk. Frankie pawed through it.

"What are you looking for?" Danny said.

"I will know it when I see it," Frankie said carefully. He pulled out a shriveled old apple.

"Amazing," said Howie. "Perhaps Isaac Newton discovered gravity with that."

"It looks old enough," Danny said.

Frankie took more stuff from the box and stacked it on the desk. Soon he had a sloppy pile of coils of wire, copper tubing, slide rules, and an early telescope.

Danny picked up the telescope. It was little more than a paper tube with a lens at each end. "Didn't Galileo invent this?"

"He did invent the telescope. But this particular telescope?" Elisa said. "I think not."

Frankie had pulled something from the box, and he was staring at in wonder. It was the head of a mechanical dog. It seemed to be riveted together from a patchwork of small, uneven pieces of metal. Its ears were two more flaps of metal. Its eyes were thin sheets of glass, cloudy with age. Its teeth looked real but could have been chunks of finely sculpted rock.

"Wow," said Danny softly as Frankie turned the thing from side to side. "Hey look! It says something inside one of the ears!"

Frankie turned the head so that he could read the engraved words, then wiped away the years of grime with his thumb. Suddenly he froze.

"What does it say?" Howie asked.

Frankie began to shake. Elisa took the head from him and blinked many times before she spoke. At last, in an astonished voice that she barely kept under control, she said, "It says BARON VICTOR FRANKENSTEIN."

Chapter Five

A Little Family History

Everyone but Uncle Emeric was stunned. Danny had to explain to him that Frankie and Elisa were relatives of the late great Baron.

"I should have known," Uncle Emeric said as he touched either side of his neck.

"How did it get here?" Howie said.

"Where did the Transylvanian Export Company get any of these things?" C.D. said as he gestured at the pile of scientific curiosities.

No one, not even Uncle Emeric, had an answer to that question.

Frankie took the head back from Elisa and turned it over. Inside was a mass of wires and tubes and coils and clunky-looking electronic gear. Frankie set the head on the desk and began to gently tug on the wires to see where they went.

"Wait," Uncle Emeric said. "I am not paying you to investigate mysteries of science. Not even if they are family mysteries. You have stock work to do. Have you finished unloading the crate?"

Frankie admitted that they had not.

"Please proceed. And do not forget to properly dispose of the packing material." He herded C.D. and Howie back to his office.

None of them had their minds on their work. They discussed the dog head while they continued to pull boxes from the crate. Frankie said nothing. He occasionally stopped working entirely and stared into space.

They finished the crate and carefully threw away the packing material. For the rest of the morning, Uncle Emeric had Frankie, Elisa, and Danny count boxes. It was boring work, but Uncle Emeric said that it was necessary for him to keep track of his stock. The morning stretched like taffy. At one point Frankie said, "The clock is broken."

"Sure seems that way," Danny said. "This is worse than spending a spring afternoon in school."

At last noon arrived. Uncle Emeric bought everybody hot dogs and sodas for lunch. Frankie chewed each mouthful for a long, long time. He was lost in thought while the others made jokes around him.

When they were done eating, the kids began to dress for the cold weather outside. Uncle Emeric gave each of them an envelope with a check inside it. Then he gave Frankie a box and some packing material so that he could take the dog head home. "You see," said Uncle Emeric. The stringy packing material rustled as he pulled a handful of it from the box. "Nothing more exotic than shredded newspaper."

While Frankie was packing the head, Barbara came in, still carrying her Snuggly Mutt, Doc, under her arm. "What's that?" she asked when she saw the mysterious shape Frankie was wrapping.

Frankie did not answer, so Howie said, "It is the head of a dog that once belonged to Baron Victor Frankenstein."

"Oh, yuckers," said Barbara and made a face.

"It's not a real dog, you dodo," Danny said. "It's just mechanical."

"What are you going to do with it?"

Elisa said, "We are going to take it home and make it work." She smiled. "I think that at last Frankie has found a project that satisfies him."

"Wait a minute," Barbara said. "You said we were going to buy yarn this afternoon."

"Yarn?" said C.D.

"You know," Barbara said. "Like thick hairy string. Mrs. Bumpo, our Girls' Pathfinders counselor, wants us to make yarn dolls for sick kids in hospitals."

"B-o-o-ring," Elisa said. She and Barbara laughed like conspirators.

"Anyway," Barbara said, "the only way for anybody in Mrs. Bumpo's troop to get her Public Service merit badge is to make a zillion dolls. So that's what we have to do." She fixed Elisa with a steely eye. "And you promised we would go shopping when you got off work."

"But," said Elisa, "I want to see what Frankie makes of the head."

"You promised," Barbara said. There was a little whine in her voice, so Danny knew that Elisa didn't have a chance. When Barbara made that sound, she got her way or there was trouble.

Evidently Elisa knew about the whine, too, because she glanced at Danny. Danny shrugged. Elisa said, "All

49

right," and the two of them went off together discussing yarn.

Danny said, "Can I come to your house, Frankie? I'd like to help."

"Me, too," Howie cried.

"I also," C.D. said, as he made a little bow.

"Thank you," Frankie said.

With Uncle Emeric's permission, each of them used his phone. There was much calling of parents. Frankie wanted to know if it was all right to bring friends home. It was. Howie and Danny wanted to know if they could visit the Steins. They could. Acting for C.D.'s parents, Uncle Emeric gave him permission to go along.

Soon Dr. Stein drove up in his car, a sleek futuristic job much like the one belonging to Mrs. Stein. Only instead of being red, it was an apple green of such intensity that the car seemed to vibrate. Dr. Stein wore a tie that matched his car, along with his nice blue suit. Knobs protruded from his neck, and Danny could see where Frankie got his unruly hair.

"What is in the box?" Dr. Stein said when Howie, Danny, and C.D. had piled into the car behind Frankie.

Frankie said, "It is a surprise."

"Not an exploding surprise, I hope." Dr. Stein laughed as if he didn't believe for a minute that the box would explode.

"No. But it will surprise you. If I have a chance to work on it." Frankie studied his father, looking for a sign.

"Why would you not?" said Dr. Stein.

"Yeah," said Danny. "Why would you not?"

Frankie shrugged and shook his head.

When they arrived at the top of Holler Hill Drive, the wind vanes sticking out from the roof of the mill-shaped Stein home were turning in the cold wind.

Inside the house, Frankie strode to the elevator and waited for Danny, Howie, and C.D. When they had all joined him, Frankie said, "Laboratory," and the elevator descended.

The laboratory was an enormous room built from stone. It always looked to Danny like something out of an old horror movie, and it surprised him when things in it were in color rather than in black-and-white. Big clear electric globes illuminated hulking machines, throwing shadows that lurked everywhere.

The big old machines had points and wheels and coils. At the moment, they stood silently. But when Frankie got the place going, the machines would shoot lightning at each other. Along one wall, bubbles rose lazily through different colored liquids in tubes the size of adults. Below a hole high in the center of the ceiling was a long thick marble slab that could be tilted at any angle.

"Well," said Frankie as he carefully set the box on the slab.

"Well?" said Danny and Howie and C.D.

"Well, I have decided that first, we must do research. Perhaps we can learn something of the Baron's dog before I begin to take it apart and accidentally destroy some delicate part."

"Jolly good," said Howie.

"In the Mad Room," Frankie said.

The boys walked to the end of the laboratory and

51

down a sweeping stairway to the Mad Room, where this entire problem had begun. In contrast to the laboratory, the Mad Room was shiny, modern, and brightly lit by long fluorescent tubes.

Frankie took them to the home entertainment corner. The other boys sat on the couch while Frankie found a videotape and inserted it into the player.

"This," said Frankie, "is an unreleased movie based on the life of the real Baron Frankenstein." Frankie did not usually talk very much. He was uncomfortable, even in front of this friendly audience, and he shuffled his feet and swung his arms as he spoke. He went on, "My family made it in order to tell the real story. I have not seen it in many years and may have forgotten much. Perhaps it will give us a clue about the dog. Now," Frankie said as he pushed the PLAY button and joined the others on the couch.

Having seen the old Boris Karloff version of *Frankenstein,* Danny was unprepared for *Stitches*. The fact that some scenes were in color did not help. There was no music. A few scenes showed the microphone or members of the crew standing around in their jeans and T-shirts. Most of the crew members seemed to have knobs on their necks. A lot of the footage seemed to have been shot in the Steins' laboratory, or a place very much like it.

You could tell that some scenes had not been shot at all because occasionally a card was inserted saying that scene such-and-such was missing. If it hadn't been for the cards, Danny would not have known. What was there was boring. Maybe more boring than making yarn dolls. Danny had never made a yarn doll, so he didn't know.

According to the movie, the Baron Frankenstein was a medical student who experimented on cadavers at his medical school. Igor, his assistant, was not a weird old hunchback but a fairly normal guy. He was the Baron's lab partner. They did their homework together in the Baron's laboratory. Neither of them ever robbed a graveyard. The Baron discussed his work freely with his girlfriend, who was a nurse. At the end, the Baron and his girlfriend got married and legally adopted the monster, and the three of them strolled off into the sunset together.

When the movie was over, Danny said, "It's just not the same without the angry villagers."

"Perhaps not," Frankie said. "That may be why *Stitches* was never released."

"I found it, er, interesting," Howie said.

"Interesting. Yes," C.D. said. "But nowhere in the film is there a mention of a dog."

"Maybe the dog was in the missing scenes," Danny said.

"My thought exactly," Frankie said. "Fortunately, I have the complete script."

They went back upstairs to the laboratory. Danny, Howie, and C.D. looked around at the room as if they had never seen it before. When something has been in a movie, even a boring movie, it somehow becomes more interesting.

Frankie took a bound sheaf of papers from a filing cabinet. The corners of the sheaf were curled and dirty as if it had been well thumbed. "This is the script for *Stitches*," Frankie said. "It is a hundred and twenty pages long. Perhaps each of us can read thirty pages and see if the dog is mentioned?'' He handed out thirty pages to each of them and kept the remainder for himself. They began to read.

Danny had the part about the Baron's success animating the creature. In the old Karloff movie, the Baron was a little crazy. He rubbed his hands together and made dramatic pronouncements as he used lightning to bring the creature to life. In *Stitches,* the Baron used old-fashioned storage batteries as his source of electricity. Everything was very calm and scientific. The Baron was too busy to make speeches. He was always taking notes. There was nothing about a dog.

When he was done, Danny looked up. He and Howie traded glances and shrugged. Frankie and C.D. were still reading. A while later, Frankie looked up and said, ''Nothing?''

Howie and Danny shook their heads.

''Nothing about a dog,'' C.D. said as he continued to flip through his pages. ''However . . .''

''However?'' Howie, Danny, and Frankie said together.

''However, there is mention of a secret room.''

''Well, go on, man,'' Howie cried.

''It seems,'' C.D. said, ''that the Baron had a secret room behind the laboratory walls. There he would conduct experiments he wanted to keep secret even from his girlfriend and Igor.'' C.D. smiled. ''Evidently both of them were rather talkative.''

''Was a mechanical dog one of his big secrets?'' Danny said.

Frankie said, ''It is possible. We must find that room and investigate.''

Chapter Six

The Secret Lab of Frankenstein

The four boys looked around the laboratory with new eyes. "This is an enormous place," Danny said.

"And your ancestor was no fool," Howie said. "If he wanted to keep a laboratory secret, he probably did a good job of it."

"You are right," said Frankie. "We must return to Uncle Emeric's store and get one of those programmable electronic dowsing rods."

"What good will that do?" said Danny.

"It will send out ultrasonic signals that will bounce back. Open places like a room will make different kinds of echoes from solid rock walls."

Howie said, "I'll wager that the Baron never thought of *that*."

"Wait," C.D. said as Frankie ran to the elevator.

Frankie turned and waited.

"I may be of assistance. As perhaps you know, bats navigate by using ultrasound. I will take my bat form and find the hidden room."

"Will it work?" Danny said.

"Of course it will work," Howie said. "Capital idea."

"Please try," Frankie said. "It will save us much time."

"And," said Howie, "we will not have to explain to Uncle Emeric why we need one of his dowsing rods."

C.D. nodded. He opened his cape wide, showing the scarlet lining. He leaped into the air, and suddenly a large bat was flapping its wings where C.D. had stood.

"I'll never get used to that," Howie said.

Danny looked at him in astonishment. Howie laughed.

"There he goes," Frankie said as he pointed at C.D.

Sounding like a pair of wet hands clapping, C.D. flapped around the room. He made a screeching noise that was so high-pitched that Danny felt it, rather than heard it. C.D. dived around the room, enjoying his freedom, and then flapped against the walls, as if he were a moth trying to escape.

As Danny had noted, the laboratory was an enormous place, and it took C.D. quite a while to go over the whole room. While he worked, Danny and Howie watched Frankie pick at the inside of the dog head. "This is very interesting," Frankie said. "Far beyond its time."

"Can you make it work?" Danny said.

"I am not sure."

"Don't begin to doubt yourself now," Howie said, "with victory so near at hand."

"Sure," said Danny. "I can't think of another kid your age who could have built Monsterland."

"Certainly," said C.D. He was standing near them, his arms folded, looking as if he had never been a bat.

He was smiling. "This is no time to give up. I have found the secret room."

"Where?" said Frankie.

C.D. walked to one wall. It was no different from all the others except that a row of cylindrical machines, each as tall as C.D.'s father, stood against it. They looked like electrical mushrooms—each with wire wound around its stem and a shiny spherical cap on top.

"What are they?" Howie said.

Frankie said, "They are Tesla coils. They produce very high voltage at a very high frequency."

"What does that mean?" Howie said.

"It means," Frankie said, "big fancy sparks."

Between the Tesla coils were little tables holding strange objects that might have belonged to the Baron: stuffed alligators, ancient and dusty chemical equipment, reagent bottles, some of which still held liquid, bell jars with moldering, unidentifiable *things* under them, and rusty, ancient tools whose purpose none of them could guess.

Hanging on the stone wall were certificates from universities that had long German names, old diagrams of the human body with astrological signs all over the place, and bones of animals mounted on plaques.

"What do you suggest?" Howie said.

"In the movies," Danny said, "secret rooms always have secret doors that you open by pushing or pulling or tilting something."

Frankie nodded. "Very well," he said. "Let us begin."

The boys did as Danny had suggested. They moved anything that could be pushed or pulled or tilted. Some stuff, like the tools, was not connected to anything but bales and bales of spiderwebs. The boys dared each other to touch them. Most things would not move at all.

Howie pulled a bone that was labeled the shinbone of a small dinosaur. It was hinged at the bottom, and when it moved, it pulled a metal rod a little way out of the wall. The mechanism moved easily enough, as if it ought to do something, but the wall remained as blank as it had been before. Suddenly, three Tesla coils down, a grating noise began.

"Look," cried Danny.

The coil part of the Tesla coil rose, revealing a doorway in the remaining metal cylinder.

The boys gathered around the doorway and looked down into the dark stairwell.

"Reminds me of home," C.D. said.

"Yeah," Danny said without enthusiasm.

"Do you have any torches?" Howie said.

Danny said, "Torches would fit right in, but flashlights would give more light."

"In England," Howie said, "a torch *is* a flashlight."

"Ah. Very well," Frankie said. He ran down to the Mad Room and returned a moment later with an enormous flashlight. "It takes six D batteries," he said proudly. He did not move toward the stairway.

"Well, let's go," C.D. said.

"Yeah. Let's go," Danny said. "You have the flashlight, Frankie. You go first."

Frankie said nothing. But he switched on the flashlight, and it put out a bright beam.

"Very encouraging," Howie said.

Frankie took one step down into the Tesla coil and

stopped. Organ music began to echo up the stairs from below.

"Spooky," Danny said.

"Certainly no one could be down there," C.D. said. "Not after all this time?"

"You tell us," Danny said. "You're the one with the ancestors who won't stay horizontal."

"A thing that makes music can't be all bad," Howie said hopefully.

Frankie nodded and once more began to descend. Fighting for last place, Howie, Danny, and C.D. followed close on his heels.

The stairs twisted down into the ground like the stairs that led to the Chamber of Horrors in Mr. Price's wax museum. A layer of slimy water droplets covered the cold, wet stones. But that didn't bother Danny so much as the organ music, which continued to grow louder and more dramatic as they descended. He shivered. He told himself that he shivered from the cold.

Could there really be somebody down there? And if there was, shouldn't the boys call the police or an exorcist or something? But no. Danny continued to follow Howie, who followed Frankie. C.D. was so close he breathed on Danny's neck.

There was a large wooden door at the bottom of the stairs. Behind it the organ music continued. To Danny it sounded as if some crazy guy were working himself up to something Danny probably would not like.

"Maybe it's locked," Howie said.

Frankie grabbed the iron ring that served for a door-knob and pulled. The door squeaked a little, but it came open easily. Frankie stopped when the door was open just a crack and looked back at his friends. Like Howie and C.D., Danny nodded. Stupid. Stupid. The door squealed as Frankie pulled it open.

The organ music poured over them. Frankie swung his flashlight around the small room beyond the door. It was obviously another laboratory, but without most of the equipment that the upstairs laboratory had.

Against one wall stood a pipe organ. But nobody and nothing was sitting on the bench before it. The thing was covered in dust and spiderwebs. Danny guessed it would need a good cleaning, at the very least, before it would produce music.

Were they hearing ghost music? Not just music played by ghosts, but the ghost of music itself? Danny decided this was not the case. The music did not seem to be coming from the organ, but just filled the room.

The organ music reached a climax and ended. A man began to talk and Danny jumped. Then he listened to what the man was saying. He was asking for money to support fine organ performances like the one just heard on noncommerical radio.

"That sounds like Raymond Cavelero!" C.D. said. "He is an announcer on that public radio station that plays classical music."

"Indeed," said Frankie. He had his ear against one wall. "We must be listening to my mother's radio in the kitchen. The sound is conducted by the stone walls."

Danny let out a breath he hadn't realized he was holding. "Good old Raymond Cavelero," he said.

On a slab in the center of the room was a shape

covered by a sheet. As Frankie grabbed the sheet with both hands, Danny said, "I wonder if this is one of those things Man was not meant to know."

Frankie did not even pause to consider Danny's remark. He pulled the sheet, raising a cloud of dust. The boys coughed and sneezed and waved their hands in the air. Through the dust and his sneezing, Danny saw that under the sheet were the body and legs and tail of a mechanical dog, all in pieces.

"So," said Frankie as the dust settled. He rubbed his nose, then picked up the ancient, leather-bound book that lay on the slab next to the pieces of dog. As he carefully looked through it, Frankie said, "It is the Baron's notebook. Come. Let us take Bruno upstairs."

"Bruno?" Danny said.

"According to this book, that is the name of the dog."

Frankie carefully collected the parts of the dog into the sheet, and cradling the bundle as if it were a child, he led the way back up to the main laboratory.

Frankie laid the parts of Bruno's body on the slab next to its head. He arranged the legs and tail roughly the way they would go if everything were connected. "Now," said Frankie as he began to gently probe the head and then to poke through the neckhole into the chest of the mechanical dog.

Occasionally, he asked Howie or Danny or C.D. to hold something for him while he looked at something beneath it, but mostly he worked in a fog, not even aware that his friends were there. Over and over again, he hummed the organ music they'd heard.

After a while, he had a bunch of wires and a row of brass components laid out on the slab along with the head and the body parts. One of the components was as big as a fist, some of them looked like marshmallows, but most of them were no larger than a matchbook. All of them were carefully made of even tinier parts. With satisfaction, Frankie surveyed what he had done, and said, "Will someone get me Monsterland? It is in the Mad Room."

"I'll get it," Danny said, already on his way. He ran across the lab, then leaped down the sweeping stairway, two steps at a time. Monsterland was standing by itself on a table. Danny grabbed it and was back at the slab in a moment. "Here," he said.

"Thank you," Frankie said. He opened the back of the game and looked inside. Danny could not make head or tail of what he saw. Except for three boards covered in small electronic parts that looked like insects, the box was empty. "Ah," said Frankie as he reached in and pulled one of the boards out. Then, carefully, with a pair of plastic tweezers, he pulled loose one of the little electronic insects and held it up for all to see.

Frankie said, "This is the main memory chip of Monsterland. There is not another like it in the world. With it, I will make this mechanical dog do things that the Baron Frankenstein never dreamed of. I will prove to my parents that I am as bright as any of my ancestors."

Suddenly the chip slipped from the tweezers and fell. It clinked as it hit the stone floor. "Look out," cried Frankie. "Don't step on it." They each took a step back and Danny heard a sickening crunch. Everyone froze.

Then, slowly, fearfully, Frankie got down on his

hands and knees. A second later, he groaned and leaned back to sit on the floor. He seemed to be on the edge of tears. Danny and the others got down to look. They saw a spot of pulverized glass and crushed metal.

"Well," said Howie, "you can build another one."

"It will take weeks," Frankie said. "By that time, it could be too late."

Chapter Seven

Barbara's Faithful
Snuggly Mutt, Doc

The boys sat on the floor for a while in a funk. Their brains were filled with black, impenetrable smoke that did not allow room for thoughts. C.D. pulled his thermos from the pocket inside his cape and began to suck on his Fluid of Life.

Danny knew that Frankie had had a tough time over the last week, and losing the chip was the final blow. Even now, Danny was not convinced that Frankie and Elisa were candidates for the junk heap. But there was always a chance that Frankie was right about that. After all, Frankie was a pretty smart guy. And they'd all heard the conversation between Dr. and Mrs. Stein. It was certainly open to some strange interpretations. And if Dr. Stein was unhappy with Frankie's schoolwork anyway—well, you never knew about grown-ups.

Maybe none of this was the question. The question was: If Frankie thought he was right, now that all other possibilities were cut off, what drastic thing might he do to save himself?

Without changing his expression, Frankie said, "I have an idea."

The boys looked at him.

"I need the main memory chip from Barbara's Snuggly Mutt."

"Good luck," Danny said.

"If you need it," C.D. said, "we will get it somehow."

"I don't care how much we need it. Barbara's still my sister. I don't know what I'd tell Mom and Dad if something happened to her."

"Fear not," C.D. said.

The elevator dinged, announcing that someone was about to arrive. "Here's your chance to try something," Howie said. "That's probably them now."

The elevator doors slid open and Elisa and Barbara marched in. Each of them was carrying a bulgy bag with the words YARN WORLD on the side. In her other hand, Barbara clutched her Snuggly Mutt, Doc.

"You should see the stuff we got," Barbara said as she pulled a big skein of purple yarn from her bag. "I hope Mrs. Bumpo is happy with it." When she saw Bruno's parts laid out on the slab, she stopped with her hand still in the air.

"You found the rest of the dog," Elisa said with delight.

"Indeed," said Frankie.

"You still are not happy," Elisa said.

Howie was about to say something, but Danny elbowed him in the arm. Howie said, "His name is Bruno," and gave Danny a dirty look.

Barbara was investigating Bruno's innards. She said, "Where did you find the rest of him?"

"In the secret room," Danny said.

"Perhaps you would like to see it," C.D. said. He smiled, showing his fangs.

Barbara looked at C.D. suspiciously. She said, "Perhaps you'll tell me why you guys are so interested in showing it to us."

"OK," said Danny. "Don't go. It's boring. It looks just like our living room at home only the wallpaper is green instead of blue."

Barbara shook her head at that and sniffed with contempt. "Come on, Elisa. Let's take a look." Barbara dropped her bag on the slab but still held her Snuggly Mutt. Frankie showed her and Elisa the entrance through the Tesla coil and handed Elisa the flashlight. Screaming like wild animals, they ran down the stairs.

When they were gone, Danny said morosely, "We could lock them in the secret room till they agree to give us the Snuggly Mutt."

"Explain *that* to your parents," C.D. said.

"We could just take it," Howie said. He sounded uncertain.

Frankie said, "I do not like threatening or stealing. If I do such a thing, I will deserve whatever my parents have in mind for me."

"What will we do then?" Howie said.

"Then," said Frankie, "I will have to convince her."

Someone was coming down the stairs from the main house. Quickly Frankie threw the sheet over Bruno, the Baron's mechanical dog, and the boys leaned casually against the slab. As far as Danny could tell, the thing under the sheet could have been anything from a log to the motor of a UFO.

Frankie's father walked into the lab. "Hello, boys," he said. "Staying out of trouble?"

"Yes, sir," they all said together.

"I thought I heard Elisa come in," Dr. Stein said.

"She is not here," Frankie said. Which was more or less true.

"If you see her, please tell her we have much to discuss."

"Oh?" Frankie looked stricken.

Dr. Stein shook his head and laughed. "It seems that when she joined the Girls' Pathfinders, the entire family joined, too."

Frankie smiled.

"Hard at work?" Dr. Stein said as he pointed to the slab.

"Just something for school," Frankie said.

"Let me know if you need some help with it."

"Why should I need help?"

"Keep your temper, Frankie. Even *you* will occasionally need help."

"Yes, sir."

"Nice to see you, boys," said Dr. Stein. He crossed the laboratory and walked back up the stairs.

When he was gone, Danny said, "He doesn't seem like the kind of guy who would dismantle his children."

"You are right. But you heard what he said about my needing help. If he is so unhappy with me, who knows what he will do?"

To Danny, the evidence hardly seemed conclusive. Frankie pulled the sheet off Bruno and began to once again organize the mechanical dog's parts.

Danny heard stomping on the stairs, and soon Barbara

and Elisa returned to the laboratory. "Boy, what a creepy place," Barbara said. "You found the rest of the dog down there?"

"We did."

"How did you know where to look?" Elisa said.

"It is a long story," Frankie said. "I will tell you later. Right now, I must discuss an important matter with Barbara."

"What sort of important matter?"

Frankie did not answer. He swung his hands and worked his mouth as if he were trying to think of something to say.

"Must be some important matter," Barbara said. "Look, I have a lotta yarn dolls to make. I'll see you guys. 'Bye, Elisa." She picked up her bag and walked toward the elevator.

Frankie said, "I need the main memory chip from your Snuggly Mutt."

Barbara stopped, then turned around slowly. "Huh?" she said. She was clutching Doc against her chest.

"I need the memory chip."

"Why?"

"You see, I must rebuild Bruno. But I want the dog to be better than it was. I want it to bark and respond to my voice the way your Snuggly Mutt does."

"Why?"

"Why? Why? Why?" Frankie got frantic. He began to jump around with such enthusiasm the kids backed off to give him room.

"You see this leg?" Frankie cried. Like a maniac, he picked up one of Bruno's legs and shook it in Barbara's face. The joints of the leg made a strange, soft, rattling

69

noise. "If I do not prove to my mother and father that I am brighter than the Baron Frankenstein, this is all that will be left of me! And this!" He picked up another leg and shook it. "And this!" He picked up the tail and shook it.

Frankie ran around the laboratory waving the legs and the tail above his head. "They will take me apart! They will reprogram my brain." He dropped the legs and the tail with a clatter. He grabbed his head in both hands and looked around the lab as if he had never seen it before. Melodramatically he said, "Who am I? Where am I? What is what?" He staggered toward Barbara, still gripping his head. Barbara backed away.

Danny himself was astonished at Frankie's performance. Usually Frankie was the quietest one of the group, speaking in the fewest possible words, and then only when he had something important to say. If he was running around like a chicken without a head, screaming and carrying on, he must be even more upset than Danny had thought.

Frankie seemed suddenly to be aware of what he had been doing. Embarrassed, he turned away from Barbara, got the legs and the tail from where he'd dropped them, and returned to the slab. "You get the idea," he said.

Barbara nodded. "In other words," she said, "you want to do to Doc what you say your father wants to do to you."

Frankie thought about that for a moment. This was obviously a new idea for him. He even smiled a little. He said, "Yes. I suppose I do."

"Frankie is very honest," Elisa said.

"I suppose," Barbara said slowly, "that when all this

is over, somebody can restuff Doc and sew him up again. Even without his memory chip, he'd still be good to cuddle with.''

"Capital idea," Howie said.

C.D. bowed and said, "My father is an expert tailor. I am sure that he would be delighted.''

Barbara surprised everybody by hugging C.D. "You guys are wonderful,'' she said. "I don't know why I ever thought you were monsters.''

"All depends on your definition,'' Howie said.

"Yeah,'' Danny said. "You ought to ask Stevie Brickwald's opinion sometime.''

"Now *there* is a monster,'' Elisa said, and everybody laughed.

"OK, then,'' Barbara said. "Just as long as we understand each other. What's in it for me?''

"In it?'' Frankie said.

"My gosh, Barb,'' Danny cried, "you see how important this is to Frankie. How can you ask a question like that?''

Elisa added, "It is hardly the sort of question a Girls' Pathfinder would ask under the circumstances.''

"I was just asking,'' said Barbara. "It doesn't really matter, I suppose. Still, if I'm giving up the brain of my Snuggly Mutt, I ought to get something. It's only fair.''

"Maybe she's right,'' Howie said.

"Maybe,'' C.D. said, unconvinced.

Elisa thought for a moment and said, "Suppose I made half of your yarn dolls?''

Barbara thought for a moment. Frankie watched her with such intensity that Danny half-expected her to have two little holes burned into her. At last Barbara cried, "Sold!"

Frankie put out his hand. Barbara shook it. "No, no," Frankie said gently. "Give me the Snuggly Mutt." Barbara looked at him. It was a solemn moment. Barbara stroked her Snuggly Mutt, Doc, one last time, and sniffling just a little, she handed him over to Frankie.

Frankie put Doc on the table. From a stack of drawers beneath the slab he took a scissors, held it over Doc, and said, "We begin."

Barbara turned away. Then she turned back again to watch in fascination as Frankie lowered the scissors toward Doc's body.

Chapter Eight

Frankie Throws the Switch

"You're not going to cut Doc without putting him to sleep first," Barbara said. She sounded shocked.

"Barbara," Danny said with disgust.

"It is only a stuffed animal," Elisa said gently.

"No, no," Frankie said. "She is right. What would you suggest, Barbara?"

She thought for a moment and said, "Hot chocolate? That always puts me right to sleep."

"Perhaps some chocolate powder?" Elisa said. "I believe there is some in the Mad Room kitchen."

"OK. I guess Doc can handle it."

"Absolutely," Danny said.

While Elisa was getting the chocolate powder, Frankie built a face mask from a funnel and a length of rubber hose. Everybody tried to look very serious for Barbara's benefit, but Howie kept snickering. Barbara ignored him.

Elisa came back with an individual packet of powdered chocolate milk—just add water.

"We will not add water," Frankie said.

"Because the powder acts faster, right?" Barbara said.

"Exactly." Frankie put the funnel over Doc's muzzle and gently tapped the chocolate powder into the open end of the tube. He tapped a little more in. "Enough?" he said.

"One more tap," Barbara said, "just to make sure."

Frankie tapped again.

"OK," Barbara said.

Frankie took away the face mask and the chocolate. Barbara nodded and Frankie carefully snipped open her Snuggly Mutt, Doc. He pulled out a fistful of cotton batting and came to a small block of hard rubber. He turned the ends of the block in opposite directions and it fell into two pieces. Inside were a number of chips which Frankie studied carefully.

With his plastic tweezers, he pulled one of them loose from its metal clip. Instead of holding it up, he set it down immediately in a little plastic box and closed the top. Danny could see it in there, looking like a tiny street map of a futuristic city.

Everyone let out a breath.

"Brave little doggie," Barbara said.

"Indeed," said Frankie. "First we must analyze the chip so that I know what its electronic needs are. After that, I can build Bruno around it." He picked up the small box and carried it quickly down into the Mad Room. The group rushed to follow him.

By the time Danny got there, Frankie had once more picked up the chip in his tweezers and set it inside a kind of drawer in the side of a computer. He closed the drawer with a click, and a red light went on.

Frankie said, "The computer will now take seconds to do the analysis that would take me weeks to do alone." He began to type into the computer. Columns of numbers appeared on the screen, disappeared one by one, only to be replaced by more numbers.

After a while, Frankie stopped typing, but the columns of figures continued to come and go. Come and go. Frankie studied the screen carefully. No one said a word. Soon the columns of numbers disappeared for the last time and the word WORKING appeared where they had been.

"It will be a few minutes," Frankie said.

The computer beeped, calling everyone's attention back to the screen, where a diagram of the chip was growing. The computer laid out long stripes that split and twisted around and ended with big dots. Next to each dot was a long serial number.

Frankie said, "You see, the computer is telling me all about the chip." The computer finished the picture, and Frankie began to type again. "I want Bruno to use regular batteries and other modern components as well as what the Baron has supplied," he said. Pretty soon the diagram of the chip shrank to one corner of the screen, and the screen listed all the things Frankie would need to rebuild Bruno using the Snuggly Mutt chip.

Danny recognized some of the words: *chip, resistance, voltage,* but had no idea how any of this stuff might go together. He also didn't know where they would get it without visiting Uncle Emeric's store and spending a ton of money.

Frankie pushed one final button, and a laser jet printer

began to hum. Seconds later, Frankie had paper copies of the diagram of the chip and the list of components.

"Where will you get all that stuff?" Danny said.

Frankie looked around the Mad Room and said, "I am sure I must—how do you say it? I have seen this word in *Robinson Crusoe*."

"What could a guy living by himself on a desert island possibly have to do with electronic dogs?" Barbara said.

"I saw the movie once," Danny said. "Robinson Crusoe lived by himself for a long time till he found this other guy named Friday, and at the end they fought off a bunch of cannibals."

"Cannibals. That is it," said Frankie.

Danny was horrified. All his worst fears came together in that one word. "You don't mean—"

"What?" said Frankie, who was already thinking about something else. "I will take a bit from here and a bit from there and build something else from the bits."

Danny watched with relief as Frankie began to roam the room, studying his video games. They were big floor models, the kind you might see in an arcade at a shopping mall.

Eventually, Frankie used his plastic tweezers to pull pieces out of "Zombie Nights," "Mummy Madness," "Whirlpool," and "Interstellar War Zone." He collected the bits of metal and quartz in an envelope and took them back to the lab along with his printouts of the chip and the components.

Danny touched Elisa's arm, and the two of them hung back while the rest of the kids hurried up the stairs to the laboratory. Danny whispered, "What will happen if Frankie really isn't as smart as the Baron?"

"Frankie will be distressed."

"Yeah, but will your dad take him apart?"

"I do not know for sure. But I think not." Elisa smiled and went on. "For one thing, Mama would not let him."

"Doesn't Frankie know that?"

"He knows, but he is so upset that he does not believe."

They didn't say another word as they walked up the stairs. Danny wondered how he got himself into these messes.

Frankie was setting out big candelabras, each of which held five thick, drippy candles. "What are those for?" Danny said. "The light globes give plenty of light."

"Tradition," Frankie said as he placed a candelabra at each end of the slab.

"Very important," Elisa said. "The Baron would have wanted it this way."

Sure, Danny thought. If you're building a monster, or even a monster pet, you have to do things right.

It was fascinating to watch Frankie and Elisa light the candles. One of them would point at a candle and zap a small lightning bolt at it from one finger. B-z-z-z-i-p-it! and the candle was lit.

"Pretty neat," Danny said.

"Thank you. Will you assist me?" Frankie asked Elisa.

"Of course."

From a cabinet, Elisa took a pile of carefully folded clothing. She helped Frankie put on a long white lab coat that tied with strings, front and back. Over this Frankie wore a rubber apron that covered him from neck

to shoe tips. He put on safety goggles, and then thick rubber gloves that reached to his elbows, the kind a villain in a comic book might wear.

"Face mask?" said Howie and offered Elisa a clean handkerchief. Elisa looked inquiringly at Frankie.

Frankie said, "I do not think that will be necessary." He rubbed his hands together while he studied the equipment and components and pieces of dog before him. Suddenly, as if he had made a decision, he set to work.

Frankie worked carefully, but quickly. He used wires to connect the Baron's old clunky electronic stuff to the chips that had been cannibalized from the video games. Everything that Frankie stuffed into Bruno looked like some kind of bush from space, with small metallic fruits hanging from wiry branches.

The whole production was a lot sloppier than the insides of the Snuggly Mutt. But, Danny told himself, that didn't matter. As long as Frankie knew where everything went, and it all fit inside Bruno's body, neatness did not count.

Frankie fitted on the legs and the tail. It took longer to connect the head to the body because the head contained so much thinking stuff—including the chip from the Snuggly Mutt—that would control the rest of the dog.

Frankie worked. The candles sputtered and popped. Danny and the others sat down and stood up again. Howie suggested that they go play in the Mad Room, but nobody else wanted to. They didn't want to miss anything.

"Now please," Frankie said and Danny jumped. It

had been a long time since anybody had said anything. "If you are near apparatus, please go somewhere else. I am about to energize Bruno."

Danny saw that he was leaning against a metal hoop the size of a wagon wheel, with sharp points sticking out from it. He hurriedly left it and joined the other kids around the slab. Bruno was all in one piece, but lying on his side. He did not look quite real because he was all sharp angles and precise curves. Yet he was the proper size and shape for a dog, and in the flickering candlelight, he seemed to be moving.

Frankie connected a big clip, the kind that mechanics use to recharge car batteries, to the knobs on either side of Bruno's neck. "Now," he said, "if you will please to blow out all the candles." Danny and Howie and C.D. and Barbara each blew out one or two of them. Frankie and Elisa took care of the ones at either end of the slab.

"Good," said Frankie. "We want no fires." He walked to where an enormous lever protruded from the wall.

"Wait a minute," Barbara cried. She snatched up Doc from the slab and hugged him tightly. "We're OK now," she said.

Frankie nodded. "And now," he said, "we see." He yanked the lever down.

The room came alive with electricity. Lightning zapped everywhere. The thing Danny had been leaning on spun and crackled as it shot off jagged bolts. Time and again, sparks flashed and rose with a hum between the insectlike antennae of the machine, only to break and disappear with a loud crack.

The entire room seemed to flash in and out of existence as arcs flared and were gone. Bubbles rose frantically in the big tubes of liquid. The slightly chemical smell of ozone, the same invigorating smell that fills the air after thunderstorms, now filled the laboratory. Static electricity made the tiny hairs on the back of Danny's neck stand up.

Frankie pushed the lever back into position, and suddenly the laboratory was quiet but for a spinning piece of apparatus whistling more slowly as it slowed down. Then even that stopped. After all the sound and fury, the laboratory seemed much quieter than it had before.

Slowly, nearly on tiptoe, the kids approached the slab. The dog looked the same as it had before Frankie pulled the switch. "Now," said Frankie, "we see if it works." He reached for a toggle switch on the back of the dog's neck.

"Aren't you going to disconnect the cables first?" Danny said.

"Not first. First we see if it works." Frankie reached forward, and this time nobody stopped him. He flicked the switch. An enormous fork of lightning jumped across the room and everything went black.

Chapter Nine

Listening with Both Ears

"Oh my gosh!" and "What's happening?" Barbara and Howie cried together.

Danny felt something touch him, and he jumped away. "Ooch," said somebody as Danny knocked him down. "Look out!" Danny heard flapping. C.D. must have turned into a bat and be flying around the room using his ultrasound.

"Everyone stay calm," Elisa said. She did not sound very calm herself.

Danny saw beams of flashlights poke into the darkened laboratory from the stairwell that led to the house above. "Are you all right?" That was the voice of Dr. Stein.

"The entire house is dark. What happened?" That was the voice of Mrs. Stein.

"Over here, Papa," Frankie said. "We will reset the circuit breakers."

Everything looked weird and creepy in the flashlight beams. Gigantic shadows danced on the walls as Dr. Stein crossed the laboratory. He came to where Frankie was standing and shone his light on the breaker box. Illuminated in this way, Frankie looked like a statue of himself. "Ah, now I see," Frankie said. He opened the box and flicked all the circuit-breaker switches upward.

The laboratory filled with light from the electric globes. Danny blinked at the sudden brightness. Howie was sitting on the floor near him. "Did I knock you down?" Danny said. He extended a hand to help Howie up.

"Quite all right, old man," said Howie as he bounded to his feet. "It was all part of the excitement."

C.D. flapped down next to Barbara and became a boy again. She took a step away from him in surprise and smiled shyly. Elisa was clutching the slab as if it were a life raft. Mrs. Stein was standing at the foot of the stairs. All of them, even C.D., were squinting.

Dr. Stein shut off his flashlight and said, "Well, that was just like the old days, eh, Maria?"

"Indeed it was, Viktor," said Mrs. Stein. "Frankie, what has been going on down here?"

"This," said Frankie. He walked to the slab and pointed at Bruno.

"It looks as if it is a dog," Dr. Stein said.

"It is a dog," said Frankie. "It is the Pet of Frankenstein." He folded his arms.

"Frankenstein?" both the elder Steins said together in awe and surprise.

"Yes," said Elisa. "A little project of the Baron's."

Dr. and Mrs. Stein glanced at each other, then looked back at Elisa. Mrs. Stein said, "Where did you get such a thing?"

Elisa took up the tale. She told her parents about finding Bruno's head at Uncle Emeric's store. And how this led them at last to the secret laboratory where they found the rest of the dog. Dr. Stein snapped his fingers and said, "I knew it was here someplace. Where was the doorway?"

"Third Tesla coil from the left," Frankie said.

"A very important discovery," Dr. Stein said.

"But why?" Mrs. Stein said. "Why go to all the trouble?"

"Because after Papa told me that he was unhappy with what I did in school, I heard you both talking when wires were crossed in the intercom. You said that the present generation does not seem so bright as earlier ones."

"Yes," said Dr. Stein. "So?"

"I built Bruno to prove that I am as bright as anyone in our family, even the Baron Frankenstein himself. I do not want to be dismantled or reprogrammed."

"Dismantled?" Dr. Stein said.

"Reprogrammed?" Mrs. Stein said.

"You need not look so surprised that we have figured all this out," Frankie said. "Neither Elisa nor I am stupid."

"I will fight the person who says you are," Dr. Stein said.

"You will?" Now it was Frankie's turn to be surprised.

"Of course. Your mother and I have always said that we have smart children."

"We often argue about whose side of the family your intelligence comes from."

"You do?" Frankie said.

"Absolutely," said Dr. Stein. "It comes from mine, of course—"

"Now, Viktor," Mrs. Stein said, interrupting. Neither of them seemed upset. This was obviously a private joke between them.

"Then what were you and Mama talking about on the intercom?"

"You were not speaking of Frankie and me?" said Elisa.

"Of course not," said Dr. Stein. "We were talking about orchids. They are not as brightly colored as the crop we grew in the hothouse last year."

"Orchids," said Mrs. Stein, pronouncing it carefully to make sure everybody understood.

As glumly as if they'd said they *would* reprogram him, Frankie said to Elisa, "Will you say, 'I told you so'?"

"I will think it over," Elisa said. "For now, I will only say, *dummkopf.*" She squeezed his hand to show she did not mean it.

Dr. Stein joined Frankie at the slab and put his arm around him. He said, "You don't need reprogramming. You need only to listen with both ears and not assume so much."

Mrs. Stein shook her head. "Your father made a similar mistake when he was a child. For weeks he thought that his parents would sell him to the local power company to electrify the city during emergencies. What his father really had in mind was for them to *tour* the local power plant."

Danny started to laugh but put his hand over his mouth.

"It is silly, no?" Mrs. Stein said.

"You see," Dr. Stein said as he pulled Frankie even closer. "You are a microchip off the old block."

Everybody but Frankie laughed, and then even he smiled.

"And it does not matter," Dr. Stein went on, "that the dog does not actually work. We are proud of you for having built it."

"But the dog does work," said Frankie.

"It does?" everyone else said together.

"Or it will." He wriggled out from his father's grasp and picked up a screwdriver. He opened a trapdoor in Bruno's head and made an adjustment. "The transformer," he said.

"Ach, yes," said Dr. Stein. "Of course."

Frankie closed the trapdoor and put down the screwdriver. "I am hungry," he said as if the matter of the dog had been settled.

"Turn on the dog," Elisa said.

"You think?" Frankie said. It was obvious to Danny that Frankie was not confident about what might happen.

Everyone chimed in, encouraging him to try the dog again.

Frankie breathed deeply as he thought for a moment. Without saying a word, he put his hand on the switch. He looked around, closed his eyes, and turned it on.

Immediately Bruno's tail began to beat against the slab. He stood up on all fours and shook all over as if drying himself. The clips came loose from the knobs in his neck, and he leaped onto the floor with a clank. He barked twice and wandered off with his nose to the floor.

"I don't think Bruno ever did that for the Baron," Howie said.

"See, Doc?" said Barbara as she sort of aimed her

Snuggly Mutt in Bruno's direction. "Bruno has your brain. I'll bet you two have lots in common."

"I wish my dog, Harryhausen, were here," Danny said. "He and Bruno would have a great time."

Bruno was sniffing around the furthest corners of the lab when Frankie, as an experiment, called him. Frankie was delighted when Bruno came bounding back and leaped joyfully onto each of them in turn, licking them with his dry, papery tongue.

"Down, Bruno," Mrs. Stein said. "Down. You're getting me all dirty."

He was getting each of them all dirty. It looked as if he'd been investigating the dustiest parts of the laboratory.

When Bruno leaped onto Howie, he was delighted. Through his laughter, he said, "I've never been this close to a dog before! Real dogs are afraid of werewolves."

"The perfect pet," said Elisa.

"We will talk," said Frankie.

"Talk?" said Howie, smiling as if he couldn't believe it.

"Certainly," Elisa said. "Bruno seems to like you. If your parents agree, perhaps you can have him."

Howie got down on his knees and began to pat the metal skin behind Bruno's ears. Bruno tried to climb all over him. "But you built him."

"I will build something else now," Frankie said.

As far as Danny could see, Bruno liked everybody. But Danny didn't say anything. He had never seen Howie so happy.

Mrs. Stein tried, without much success, to brush off the paw prints that Bruno had stamped all over the front of her dress. She said, "Perhaps Howie will be able to housebreak him."

"Compared to which," Danny said as he joined Howie on the floor with Bruno, "building him was easy!"

MEL GILDEN is the author of the acclaimed *The Return of Captain Conquer*, published by Houghton Mifflin in 1986. His second novel, *Harry Newberry Says His Mom Is a Superhero*, will be published soon by Henry Holt and Company. Previous to these novels, Gilden had short stories published in such places as *Twilight Zone—The Magazine*, *The Magazine of Fantasy and Science Fiction*, and many original and reprint anthologies. He is also the author of the first two hair-raising Avon Camelot adventures of Danny Keegan and his fifth grade monster friends, *M Is For Monster* and *Born To Howl*.

JOHN PIERARD is a freelance illustrator living in Manhattan. He is best known for his science fiction illustrations for *Isaac Asimov's Science Fiction Magazine*, *Distant Stars*, and SPI games such as Universe. He is co-illustrator of Time Machine #4: *Sail With Pirates* and Time Traveler #3: *The First Settlers*, and is illustrator of Time Machine #11: *Mission to World War II*, Time Machine #15: *Flame of the Inquisition*, and most recently *M Is For Monster*, *Born To Howl*, and *There's A Batwing In My Lunchbox*.